LONGING

LEROY'S STORY

R. M. GAUTHIER

To my family who have always supported me in my endeavors.
To my friends who suffered through many versions of my novel,
this book is a new piece that hopefully they can enjoy.

CONTENTS

*A*fter entering the club, I stroll through the corridors to the security office taking my customary seat in front of the monitors. It's early. The club is closed. The monitors all look like still photographs instead of the video feeds they truly are. The place is deserted—no movement—and not another soul in sight.

This is my favorite time of the day. Quiet and peaceful. To be able to witness the serenity of this place before mobs of people swarm it to enjoy a night of depravity is special to me—an enjoyment I treasure. But it still feels strange being in an empty club.

I have worked for Landon Miller, for the past five years, since the doors opened for this establishment. He found me at my former place of employment—another club. He was a client, I was an employee.

He wasn't our typical client keeping mostly to himself and spending a lot of his time observing rather than taking part. He caught my eye on his first visit because I was the head of security and had already read his application to become a new member. However, even if I wasn't privy to his file, everyone in town knew who Landon Miller was because of his rapidly growing communications company. Landon Miller was a hot commodity whom everyone wanted to know, and everyone wanted to do business with.

When we received his application, it piqued my interest. The club catered to several high society, powerful clients. Confidentiality was strictly enforced and the screening process for clients/employees was vigorous to ensure policies and standards were met. Punishment for traitors was severe to guarantee clients had a safe worry-free environment.

When Mr. Miller became a member of the club, I watched him. He oozed confidence, always wearing a three-piece suit and radiating a sense of power with ease. He's a good-looking man who could have anyone he wanted but remained alone. He never mingled, never had anyone on his arm. He came—he watched. New members usually watched other clients—it was the natural order of things. They would watch what other members did, who they were doing it with. Instead of watching fellow members, Mr. Miller watched the employees—myself in particular. The two of us kept tabs on each other for a month before he finally approached me.

In the first couple weeks I was starting to believe the rumor mills around town were true, that the elusive Mr. Miller was gay and, in the closet, but quickly dismissed that theory. He never looked at me in a suggestive manner, instead he watched me as if I were a puzzle he was trying to figure out. I struggled at times to keep my composure being under such scrutiny, but because of my military background and the training I received in the Special Forces, I had the necessary skills to handle strenuous situations. Not that this situation was all that intense—more unnerving—odder.

Security had not been my first career choice. As a younger man my choices were limited. The streets where I grew up provided limited opportunities for its younger generation. If you happened to be a smarter child, you could work to achieve a scholarship to college but for most of us those were out of reach.

The other, most obvious choice would have been to join a gang and lead a life of crime. That held no appeal either. If I wasn't killed by a rival gang or during the commission of a crime, my mother would be sure to do the honors when she found out.

During my adolescence, several young men escaped life on the streets by becoming rappers but since I didn't have a musical bone in my body that option was out too.

With limited options, I did what many other young men in my circumstances did—I joined the Army.

It gave me a steady pay-check for the first time and enabled me to send money back home to my family. My mother—who raised us as a single parent—worked hard her entire life to provide for my me and my sister. When I received my first pay-check and sent money back home it was one of the proudest moments of my life. But my mother outright refused to accept it. As an alternative, I sent it to my little sister asking her to pay for food and expenses around the house when she could.

My time in the service was spent working hard, learning everything I could and making my way up the chain of command. I was a model soldier and was rewarded when I received an offer to train in the Special Forces. My time spent training as a Special Forces officer was grueling but I endured and began a new life. After three tours of duty I was honorably discharged and returned home.

When I arrived back on American soil, I practically kissed the ground. Leaving several nightmares behind me, I hoped to return to a normal existence. How could I know the nightmare was just beginning?

CHAPTER 2

*W*hen I returned to my hometown and childhood home, I hoped to leave the nightmares behind. Instead I discovered the money sent to my sister, Tanya, was never spent on household bills. Tanya —who was supposed to be in college—was living with a low-life pimp from the neighborhood. My mother told me the story the day after I arrived.

As I sat at the kitchen table surrounded by familiarity, she revealed the entire story of what had gone on in my absence. I felt grief-stricken by the loss of happiness and the loss of innocence that our kitchen once represented.

Mother looked much older than her 47 years with dark circles under her chocolate-brown eyes and wrinkles around the edges of her eyelids. Her hair is turning gray at the temples covering up her beautiful brown hair which was always styled. Her hair is no longer styled, instead thrown up in a messy bun at the back of her head. Replacing her fashionable wardrobe choices are tattered jeans and a T-shirt. Whatever went on in my absence displayed itself by my mother's appearance. She looked exhausted.

"Leroy, Tanya made her choice, and it wasn't to follow my rules." She stirs a pot on the stove, her body stiff as a result of this conversation. She won't look at me as she speaks—tension heavy in the air.

"I don't understand, mom." I get up and go to her side. "You told me she was doing well. You told me she was in college." I place my hand over my mother's, to stop her constant stirring.

She stares into the pot for a moment and releases a breath of air before turning to face me. "She went to college, she was doing well." She turns back to the pot and continues her vigorous stirring.

I walk across the room and stand staring out the window at the backyard. Although the house, the yard, the street appears the same, everything feels different. Everything that was so big when I was little, appears so small now—it's suffocating.

"Explain it to me, mom," I whisper, while gazing out at the swing set Tanya and I played on in our youth. "How did everything go so wrong?"

I turn to my mom, but she still refuses to look at me, instead is focused on the pot of stew she is beating. My heart drops to my stomach, my throat tightens as tears prickle my eyes. I take my seat at the kitchen table once again.

"I tried, Leroy. Tanya isn't like you, she never was." She

turns the stove off and spins around to face me. "She wouldn't listen to me."

She walks to the kitchen table, pulls the tea-towel off her shoulder and lets it drop on the table in front of her as she takes her seat. She places her head in her hands, scrubs her face a few times before putting her elbows on the table. She laces her fingers together and places her chin on the back of her hands as she lets out another sigh.

"When she started going down the wrong path..." She pulls her chin from her hands, scratches her eyebrow with her forefinger as she continues to explain.

"When Tanya went to college, she had trouble right away. She didn't think she was smart enough, prepared enough. She fell into—a depression."

She picks up the tea towel and wipes her forehead. "I honestly thought it would pass. Just nervousness about a new school, new friends, not really knowing what she was doing. I wasn't too concerned." Her eyes meet mine. "I truly thought it would pass once she got used to the school and found her way. What I didn't know was that she was seeing that..." She turns her head and glances out the window. "He slipped right past me. I had no idea who she was running around with. When I found out it was that—man." She drifts off.

I think about what she's telling me. I can't comprehend the trouble Tanya had with school. She was always the smart one. Smarter than anyone I knew. It didn't make sense she would crack under the pressure. She was a strong person. Not the type of girl who would let a man run her life. I didn't recognize the girl my mother was talking about. This was not the girl who grew up down the hall from me.

"Mom, I don't understand."

Mom's head snaps to glare at me. "Of course, you don't, you weren't here," she hisses at me in a tone I have never heard from her before.

Shock courses through me as my mother's words hit me as hard as a slap across the face. She immediately drops the tea towel onto the table reaching for my hands.

"I'm sorry, Leroy. I didn't mean to snap at you."

"It's okay. You're right, I wasn't here." I lower my eyes to the table-top ashamed I let her down, that I let my entire family down.

"It's not your fault. I didn't mean it," she pleads.

"I know, ma." I squeeze her hand tight. "It's not your fault either."

We sit in silence staring at each other.

"I thought she was doing fine, but then she started changing. She wouldn't talk about school. Hardly ever came to visit and when she did, I could see it. She was slowly turning into someone else." She squeezes my hand tightly before letting go. She sits back in her chair wiping her face with the tea towel once more.

"We didn't get along at all. Fought every time she came home because I knew—Leroy. She went downhill so fast. The last time she was here—she exploded at me. Telling me to mind my own business. To stay out of her life. She told me she was leaving and never coming back, and she hasn't."

I take a few moments to process everything she's revealing. It's hard to hear. The person Mom is talking about is not my sister. Tanya is a smart, funny, witty girl who worked hard in school and loved life. The girl mom is describing—argumentative, uncaring and downright mean —is far from the sister I left when I went away.

"Where is she now?" I peek up at my mom who is now crying.

"I don't know. Last I heard she moved in with that Martin kid," Mom whispers, her eyes on the table.

And everything falls into place at the mention of Martin. I know exactly who Martin is. Small-time local drug dealer, at least he was when I was around. That would explain her behavior and her sudden change of personality.

"When's the last time you saw her?" I ask, anxiously.

"Leroy, you have to understand," she replies.

"Oh, I understand. When?" I snap, my tone harsher than I intend as my fist comes down on the table-top hard.

"Six months." My mom gazes straight into my eyes. "I tried, Leroy. I really did but the last time she came home. Well—it was bad." Mom lowers her eyes to the table, once again.

I get the distinct impression she is withholding infor- mation from me, so I probe further. "How bad?"

She raises her eyes. "I don't want to get into all of this. You just got home." She stands from her chair and walks over to stand next to me. Taking my face between her hands, she wipes my eyes with her thumbs. "We need to celebrate." She leans down and presses her lips to my fore- head. "My baby is home, safe and sound."

She returns to the stove and resumes cooking.

Discussion over.

I remain at the table, silently processing everything. Shock—I'm in shock as I try and understand how my baby sister could become involved in drugs. To get answers to the questions running amuck in my mind I need to find my sister. I'm hoping things aren't as bad as my mother believes them to be.

"Mom, did she ever give you any help with bills and stuff," I ask.

Mom whips around to glare at me. "No. How would she do that? I never made her work. School was more important."

"When you refused my money, I sent it to her instead," I stand from the chair and walk over to her. "It was to help you with the bills." I pulled my mother into a hug. "She never gave you any of it?"

Mom leaned back gazing into my eyes. "No."

It saddens me to know my sister never helped our mother. I started to wonder if I knew my sister at all. The person we discussed was nothing like the girl I grew up with or the sister I loved with all my heart. I had to find her to figure out what went wrong.

However, before any of that could happen my mother insisted on having a coming-home party, which was happening later that night at a local restaurant. All our relatives and some people from the neighborhood would be there. After all I had just learned, partying was the last thing on my mind, but my mom appeared really excited about it and I couldn't break her heart. It seemed as if there hadn't been any fun in this house in a long time. How could I deny her?

CHAPTER 3

*W*hen we arrive at the restaurant it is wall-to-wall people. At first, I'm shocked by the turn-out. I haven't seen half of these people since before I enlisted. As the night progressed, I made my way around the room, delighted by the warm welcoming that greeted me. It's staggering to know how many people have kept me in their prayers while I was overseas.

Later in the evening, my old high school buddies walk through the door.

I immediately head over to greet them.

"Adrian." I lean in to give him a one armed hug. "How's it going, man?"

"Good. Things are good." I release Adrian and lean back to look at him. "How you doing?"

"I'm good." I reach my hand out to Tyrone. "How's life." I shake his hand.

"What's with the hand-shake?" Tyrone tugs my arm and pulls me close as he slaps me on the back.

"Nothing. How's life been treating you?" I ask, returning the pat on the back.

"Good. Wife's good. Kids are great." Tyrone leans back, a smile spreading across his features.

"How many kids you got?" I ask, smirking.

"Two," Tyrone replies, returning the smirk. "I know, I know. Who would have thought?"

We all break into laughter. Tyrone was the big man on campus in high school. Dated most of the girls in our senior year, some juniors and even some freshman, too. He was not the type to settle down and have children.

After some talk about work, kids, marriage, the three of us sit at the table laughing and carrying on. I didn't want to bring the mood down, but if anyone knew what was happening with Tanya it would be these two. Leaning forward, I decide to just ask them out right.

"So, Adrian. Have you seen Tanya around?" I place my beer bottle on the table.

The laughter is immediately halted as the two exchange a look. Adrian picks up his beer bottle and brings it to his lips.

"Not for a few months." He takes a swig out of the bottle, then places it on the table. "I'm sorry, Leroy. When all the shit went down with your ma and Tanya, your ma called me to see if I could help." He gives Tyrone a sideways glance. "We went down to see Tanya, but she was so wrapped up with Martin. We didn't get far."

He picks up his bottle and takes another swig.

"What happened?" I whisper, almost afraid of the answer.

"Martin intervened. He stood in front of your sister asking what we wanted with her." Tyrone stares at me square in the eye. "We couldn't get her alone and she refused to give us the time of day."

The silence at the table is deafening as I think about everything they've shared.

Adrian clears his throat getting my attention.

"Look, Leroy. I never told your mother, but I'm pretty sure she knows anyway. Martin's got her working," Adrian explains.

He leans forward in his seat, arms crossed over the table in front of him. "I saw her one-night standing on the corner of Carlton & Dixie. I pulled up next to her and asked her to get in the car. I thought if I could get her alone —" he trails off leaning back in his seat. He scrubs his hand over his face.

"I don't know what I thought but she refused to get in the car. In fact, she threatened to call the police if I didn't leave her alone. Then, that lowlife came sauntering over and propositioned me." He picks up his bottle and brings it to his snarling lips.

"Scum-bag," Adrian mumbles before taking a swig.

"Thanks for trying and looking out for my ma in my absence," I offer them both.

"Wish we could have done more," Tyrone says.

The night ends on a higher note as we change gears to telling stories of the past eight years. I have visited over the years, but I realize those visits were few and far between. It was nice to forget about my troubles for one evening and just have fun with the guys.

CHAPTER 4

The next day found me starting a recon mission. My target—Martin and Tanya. Martin was easy. He was on the street most of the night running his whores and drug dealers. He'd gotten a lot bigger since our younger days and he had numerous—employees. But, as with everything in that world, there are always bigger fish, and nothing is ever certain.

I spent several days watching the movements of Martin and his cohorts. Figuring out who the major players are and where their loyalties stand. Although it appears there is some loyalty among the ranks, most are just string-a-longs that would give up information for a hit. Not that I planned to use that tactic to gain information. I planned to go straight to the source. I was just waiting to see what I could learn without having my presence known. Martin is an open book, conducting business where he always did, the street corner.

Tanya is a different story. There is no sign of her. In the

past week, Martin had not put her to work or even brought her with him. It's slightly unnerving having no sign of her anywhere. It made me wonder why he's hiding her. Is she hurt? Unable to work? After a week of no visual I decide its time to make my move.

I sit in a coffee shop across the street from Martin's corner and wait. An hour later, Martin takes his spot on the corner conducting business as usual. I watch him selling drugs and women all night. He closes shop and starts for home. I follow, far enough away to make certain he's heading home but not close enough that he'll sense my presence.

He arrives at his building but is approached by an obvious druggie. I almost call off my plan when the two break out into an argument. Fortunately, or unfortunately, Martin pulls a gun on the guy and shoves him away. The druggie shakes his head, turns around and staggers back down the sidewalk. Martin shoves the gun in the back of his pants and goes into the building. The gun is not a surprise to me. With my training, a gun would never stop me, so I make my way across the street and into the building.

I creep up the stairwell hoping to preserve the element of surprise. but as I arrive on Martin's floor and walk into the hallway, he's waiting for me. He's standing against the wall, one leg bent with his foot pressed against it. His arms are crossed, gun in hand aimed in my direction. He's staring directly at me as if he knew I was coming for him.

"I wondered how long it would take you," he says.

"For what," I ask, just to clarify.

"To come find me." He cocks the gun in his hand.

"You know what I want." I take a step closer to him.

"Stay right there." He waves the gun pointing it at the floor in front of me.

I halt my motions immediately. "Where is she?"

The hallway is silent. Tension is so thick you could cut it with a knife. Martin stares at me long and hard. I remain as still as possible, not because I'm afraid of him and not because he's holding a gun aimed at my head. No, I remain still because he's the only one who knows where Tanya is. I need answers before doing something I'll regret.

Martin, on the other hand, watches me closely. His glare holds me captive. He's searching for something, what that is I'm not sure. I know he's weighing the threat I pose to him because that's how he sees me—as a threat. His assessment is correct. I'm the biggest threat in his life at this time and will stop at nothing to get the answers I came for. Gun or no gun, it won't matter either way.

Suddenly, Martin withdraws his gun shoving it in the back of his pants as he pushes off the wall, turns around and unlocks the door he is standing next to.

"Coming?" he calls out as he steps over the threshold.

I remain motionless for a moment, stunned by his sudden change in demeanor. Slowly I make my way down the hall and into his apartment closing the door behind me. Martin removes his jacket and throws it over the back of the couch, pulls the gun out of the back of his pants and throws it onto the coffee table. He sits down on the couch, pulls a pack of cigarettes out of his pocket along with a lighter. He eases a cigarette out of the pack and raises it to his lips. He flips a Zippo open and strikes the wheel with his thumb. He holds the flame to the cigarette and inhales deeply then lets out a puff of smoke. He glances over to where I'm standing.

"Want one?" He lifts the pack in my direction.

"No," I reply.

He lowers the pack and lets it drop to the coffee table. The room is not how I envisioned it. In fact, it's quite homey. I assumed the place would be dirty, rundown but certainly not the neat tidy room that surrounds me. He has nice furniture, an amazing entertainment system and several photos throughout the space. It's quite surprising and not at all what I expected from the street hustler sitting in front of me.

Martin comes across as a bad ass, leather jacket, combat boots, the typical street dealer uniform. To picture him doing dishes and vacuuming his living room is something that would not have crossed my mind. Perhaps, he has a maid.

"Take a seat." He waves his hand in the direction of a chair sitting adjacent to the couch.

I slowly make my way over and take a seat. I'm caught off guard because this is not how I saw this going down. The two of us sitting in a room talking. I planned to do battle with this man but somehow, I have misjudged the situation. Or perhaps, not.

"I've been waiting for you to show up here." He takes another drag of his cigarette, smoke billowing out from his lips.

"Where is she?" I repeat my unanswered question.

"I don't know," he confesses. "Want a beer, or something?" He stands up.

I shake my head rebuffing his offer.

Martin strolls into the kitchen. I hear the refrigerator door open and bottles clanking together. I glance around the room focusing on several pictures on display. I get up and step closer to the entertainment unit where most of the picture frames are exhibited. There are several pictures of Martin and Tanya. They look—happy. In love. They look like any regular couple, but I know this to be false. They're druggies. Although looking at these photos there's no evidence of that fact. Upon further inspection, I noticed a smaller photo tucked behind the others. I pluck the frame up and I'm immediately taken back because staring back at me is a picture of me and Tanya. We're in our mother's backyard, my arm around her shoulder, and both smiling for the camera. We look so young—happy. It's hard to believe how different things are now. Hearing Martin making his way back into the living room. I spin around to face off with him.

"Tell me what the hell is going on."

Martin scrubs his face with his hand, leans over, grabs the pack of cigarettes, and lights up another one. He lets out a deep breath as the smoke escapes his mouth.

"Look, I'd feel better if you sat down for this." He waves his hand at the chair once again.

I hesitate for a moment, then walk back to the chair, sit down and wait for him to begin.

"I admit, at first Tanya was—" he hesitates, "she was a money maker. She came to me after she was already hooked. I had no part in that." He makes his point clear as he looks me in the eye. "Apparently, she had a lot of troubles at college and started using uppers to keep up with her studies and work. She fell in with the wrong crowd and the drugs became heavier and heavier. In order to afford them she got a job stripping. That's where I found her. Strung out and stripping among other things. I saw potential," his voice cuts off as he glances at the way my hands are gripping the arms of the chair.

"I knew I could make good money off her, but not while she was all drugged out." He puts his cigarette out in the ashtray and picks up his beer bottle, taking a swig.

"Of course, you could make good money. She's a good-looking girl," I snap.

"Not when I found her. She looked like hell, believe me. I don't know what I was thinking when I approached her." He lowers the bottle back to the table. "She just had something, you know. Something that made me want to help her. I wanted her out of that bar, so I convinced her to come with me. At first, she resisted but eventually I broke her down. I brought her here. Cleaned her up. She went through awful withdrawals, but we made it. She got clean."

"Then you put her to work on the streets?" I growl.

"No. Not at first. I didn't want to. She was mine. I didn't want anyone else to have her, but she wouldn't have any of it. She didn't want me." He drops his head finding interest in the floor.

His story is unbelievable.

"Your sister's one strong girl. She wanted to make her

own way. She didn't want to rely on anyone else." He smiles as he recalls his memories.

That's the first part of his story I can believe. Tanya is pigheaded. Hard to control.

"She went to work for me for a while. I didn't like it, but..." He stops abruptly.

"In order to keep her, you let her degrade herself," I bark.

"I suppose that's the way you would see it." His eyes meet mine.

"That's the way it was."

"Anyways, like I said she worked for me for a while and slowly she let me in. We became friends. We talked—a lot —about everything." He grabs the neck of his beer bottle and points it at me. "She talked a lot about you. How you left your mom and her." He put the bottle to his lips.

"I enlisted. I had a job to do," I hiss.

"Oh, I know. She knew that too. She wasn't mad, just— lost, I guess." He lowers the bottle to his lap letting it rest.

"And, you swooped in—her knight in shining armor," I laugh, humorlessly.

"Not quite. I was just someone to talk to. Someone to listen to her. I was there for her," he accuses.

"And I wasn't. Is that it?"

"That's not what I said." He abruptly slams his beer bottle on the table making a loud clang. "If you want to hear this, then you have to shut up and let me finish."

It takes everything in me to sit back and listen to this man talk about my sister. I want to rip his head off. Kill him with my bare hands. But I know I can't, not yet. I sit back and wait for him to continue.

"At first you're right, I saw how much money she could make me." He clears his throat. "But after she got clean—I don't know." His voice changes to a wistful tone. "I wanted better for her. I wanted her to go back to school, but she refused. I wanted so much more for her than this life could give her. She was having none of it though. So stubborn, I tell ya. I asked her out. A lot. But she always turned me down. That was hard for me, I'd never had that problem before. Finally, she agreed to go out with me. On a real date. And from that moment on, she never left my side. Well, until…" He trails off as he grabs his cigarette pack off the table and sits back on the couch.

Silence fills the space between us as I wait for him to carry on. When it looks like he's not intending to, I get pissed off.

"Until?" I growl, a little harsher than intended.

"Look, you have to know I had no idea what was happening. Who those people were." He raises a cigarette to his lips lighting it with his Zippo.

I'm getting tired of waiting. Tired of his long ass story. If he doesn't get to the point soon there's no telling what I might do.

"There was this guy moving in on my territory. So, I had to stand my ground, you know." Suddenly, he jumps off the couch as he swings his arms around. "When you try to take what's mine, I strike."

I stand also, coming face to face with him. Pointing my

finger into his chest as I speak through clenched teeth. "Tell me where my sister is," I demand.

"I can't," he shouts back.

"You can't, or you won't?"

"I can't, man," he speaks softly, falling back on the couch. "I don't know what happened to her. All I know is they took her." He lets out a breath of air.

My heart drops into my stomach. My head spins watching this tough guy deflate in front of my face. Something is terribly wrong here.

"What do you mean they took her?"

"Those guys who tried to take over my territory." His hand shakes as he reaches to flick his cigarette ash.

"I don't understand?" I ask, my patience running thin.

"I thought they were looking for a fight. I thought they wanted to move in on this area. But as my boys were gearing up for a battle, they took three of my girls." He puts his cigarette out before his eyes meet mine. "They snuck in here, took three of my girls, and walked back out. No one saw anything, no one did anything. We didn't even know they had done it—until," he trails off again.

My patience snaps like piano wire stretched to capacity. Anger fills every inch of my body. "Until what?"

"Until, Tanya didn't come home. She went to visit her friend one night and didn't come home," his voice is anguished. "I wasn't concerned at first. She said she'd be back around ten, but when midnight came around and she still wasn't back, I hit the streets. I went everywhere I could think of, had all my men on the lookout for her. It was like she just disappeared. Her friend, the one she was meeting, said she never showed up. We searched all night but came up empty-handed." He gazes up at me. "Honestly, I thought she went back to your mother. I almost felt—relieved that she finally listened to me and went back home."

I sat down on the edge of the chair waiting for him to continue.

"I went to see your, mother," his gaze finds mine.

I raise an eyebrow encouraging him to continue. I can't fathom the idea of this man being anywhere near my sister, the thought makes me sick to my stomach. But now, he's talking about my mother and it's taking all that I am not to pin him against the closest wall and end his life.

"She was less than happy to see me. Practically chased me off her doorstep with a broom. Forceful woman, that one. I can see where Tanya gets it from. Anyways, after she settled and put the broom down, we had a talk. She told me that Tanya was like that—a drifter. She thought Tanya had met someone else and run off with him. For a moment it made sense because had she found someone else, she would have to run. Or at least she would think she had to run. After leaving your mother's I was almost convinced. I was pissed, sure, but I didn't plan on doing anything about it." His gaze falls to the coffee table as he reaches for his pack of cigarettes once more.

I think about his revelation and it suddenly dawns on me what he's saying. "You didn't plan anything? What is that supposed to mean? What did you do?"

"Nothing," he says, a little too quickly. "Look, when I came back home a couple of my men started telling me that my girls were missing. Two to be exact. I knew in my gut that this was no coincidence and it was all linked. Again, the search was on but for three girls now. We searched up and down for any sign of them but came up empty-handed.

"Then, one of my men told me that a couple of outsiders were trolling the area the week before. He had dealt with them and thought they had moved on, so he never bothered to mention it to me. He paid for that one." He takes a drag of his cigarette and a cloud of smoke surrounds him as he breathes it out.

He clears his throat and shifts in his seat before glancing over at me again. "I followed that lead and ended up at this kink club across town. My girls weren't there but I did find out who took them." He puts his cigarette out in the ashtray as I hold onto what little patience I have left.

"This club—I mean—I had heard about these clubs popping up around the city, but I've never been to one. Apparently, the guy that owns them is some Italian dude who everyone is afraid of. I wasn't though, so I went straight down there to find my girls. Unfortunately, the farthest I got was the front door. They knew who I was immediately and wouldn't let me in. I staked the place out for two weeks but never saw any of my girls." He sits back on the couch, shoulders slumped, defeat written all over his features.

I almost felt bad for him. Almost. I didn't know what to make of the situation. Here's this gangster, bad ass, who wouldn't think twice about killing anyone—there's no doubt about that—sitting with such disgrace clouding him. None of this makes any sense.

"Believe me, I thought about going over there Scarface style but with no sightings of my girls and not a clue where they might be, it seemed pointless." He reaches for yet another cigarette.

"So, you just gave up?" my voice raises slightly.

"No. Not right away." He lights his cigarette. "I had my guys watching the joint, and we weren't the only ones apparently. Wallace over at the 54th had guys watching the place too. Evidently, he had girls go missing. We watched for weeks with no sighting of any of the girls. Eventually, I just went in the place demanding to see the person in charge. Man, those guys were—" He trails off, looking anywhere but at me.

"What? They were what?"

"I'm a pretty tough dude, you know that. I don't back down from anyone," he shouts as he stands up pointing a finger at me. He flops back down on the couch. "Anyone." He glares at me. "But—"

"But, what?"

"These guys were different. They aren't your regular street hustlers. They're well organized, controlled, and refined. They aren't running around in street clothes. They wear designer suits, drive high-end cars and hang with the upper class. You wouldn't believe who some of the members of this club are—"

I cut him off immediately. "What do you mean members?"

"The club is different. You can't just walk in off the street. You have to be a member," he replies. "Look, Leroy. I tried everything, had everyone I know looking for them, but—" he trailed off.

"So again, you just gave up?" I repeat a little louder than necessary.

"Yeah. Okay. I just gave up," he shouts, as he stands up.

The room goes quiet.

Martin walks over to the window and looks out. I sit thinking about everything he revealed.

He turns around and looks at me.

"Man, it wasn't like I could call the police or anything. My back was up against a wall." He looks back out the window again. "There was nothing I could do."

Silence blankets the room once more. Both of us lost in thought. His voice startles me.

"That's why I went to see your mom." He saunters back over taking his seat. "I thought she could do something, you know. Call the police. Report her missing—something," he says, pleading.

"You're going to take me to that club," I commanded, leaving no room for argument. "I'm going to find out what happened to Tanya." I stand and make my way to the apartment door, calling over my shoulder. "Come on." I reach for the handle.

"I already told you, we can't get in," Martin responds as he walks up behind me.

"Don't worry about that." I pull the door open and step over the threshold. "I have a plan."

CHAPTER 5

The car is silent the entire drive. Martin attempted to argue about riding with me, but there was no way he was getting out of showing me this club. I didn't trust him to drive. He continued to gaze out the passenger window as the neighborhood passed us by. The only words spoken were his directions.

Once we arrive at the club, I park down the road along the curbside and kill the engine. The distance gives me a clear view of the front door but remain far enough to go undetected. Martin's been edgy since our arrival making me wonder what really happened at this club. His glare remains glued to the building. I observe the building and Martin attempting to calculate what is making him so anxious. For a street hustling, drug-dealing pimp, he sure appears—afraid. It's unnerving sitting in this car with him.

The building itself is nondescript. There are no windows only red brick for as far as the eye can see. In front of a wooden, windowless door a man in a three-piece suit stands guard. He's a tower of a man standing at six-foot-six inches tall, but most notably are the bulging muscles under his suit. He's wearing an ear piece and keeps talking into the sleeve of his jacket. It let me know he is in constant contact with the people inside.

I keep most of my attention on the doorman, but every so often Martin shifts in his seat gaining my attention. The longer we sit, the more anxious he becomes, his behavior not at all suited to the rough, tough guy of our neighborhood. His whole demeanor changed the minute we pulled up to this club. The tension in the car is heavy. We have only been here a half hour and haven't really seen any activity. But Martin can hardly remain still, all his attention is still focused on the door and the man standing at it. Abruptly, he turns to look at me.

"Look man, as much as I'd love to sit and chat with you all night, I have a business to run."

I shoot him a glare that shuts him up at once. His gaze returns to the club and I observe the color literally draining from his face. I return my attention to the club. A car has pulled up in front of the door and two men are just reaching the doorman. They all shake hands as they speak to each other.

"Who are they?" I whisper my gaze remaining on the club.

Martin is silent. When I glance over at him, he seems frozen as he stares at the men.

"Martin," I growl louder.

He finally snaps out of it as he looks in my direction.

The expression on his face is one of complete terror. "Who are they?"

Martin swallows, and I watch his Adam's apple bobbing. He clears his throat. "Ah, that's the owner." He points to the shorter man with black hair. "And the other guy is his brother," he replies, a slight shake in his voice. He swallows once again as he scrubs his hand across his face. His entire frame has a slight tremor that he's desperately struggling to hide. I return my focus back to the club.

The 'owner' is a small man, standing at about five feet nine inches maybe ten. He has black shoulder length hair, a pale complexion and wears a three-piece suit, *designer* by the looks of it. Hardly, your typical gangster from the neighborhood. His brother is much the same, only bigger, standing toe-to-toe with the doorman. Their interaction lasts mere minutes before the doorman grabs a hold of the handle and swings the door open. He holds it wide open while the two men stroll inside.

I glance over at Martin, who visibly relaxes once the men are out of sight.

"What really happened in there?" I point over to the club.

Martin hides his face from me but not before I can recognize his defiant expression as he looks out the passenger side window. My question goes unanswered as the car becomes silent. And, as I'm thinking of a way to get him to answer me, he gazes back at the club.

"When my boys and I went in there, guns at the ready, preparing for war, these guys..." he points at the doorman, "...were ready. Took us down in seconds. They had us disarmed, face down on the floor in mere seconds." His gaze returns to the passenger side window again, taking a moment before he continues.

"The owner, Alistair, had us taken to a back room," he stops speaking abruptly, rubs his face with his hands, and then steels himself, looking me straight in the eye. "Look, we had a run-in. I was warned to stay away, or they would hurt her. They would kill her, Leroy. So, I did—" he mumbles, as he looks away from me again, "I stayed away."

I wanted to probe further and find out exactly what happened here. What he is so afraid of? But the panic is coming off him in waves and I know there will be no further explanations tonight.

My thoughts are interrupted by a commotion at the door to the club. As my gaze focuses back to the front of the club a blond man is trying to enter but is being blocked by the doorman. The doorman folds his arms over his chest taking an immovable stance. The blond guy stands maybe five-feet eleven inches, has his hair slicked back in a ponytail. He is wearing dress pants and a sweater, but he looks rough, most likely a druggie. He is talking dramatically, waving his arms about, but the doorman stands his ground.

The door to the club swings open, and the owner appears. He is next to the blond guy in seconds putting his arm around the guys shoulder and their heads together. They speak for a few minutes and I make note of how the owner keeps patting the other guys shoulder. When they break apart, the blond man disappears down the street without even glancing back. The owner turns to the doorman who is standing with the door to the club held open. The owner nods his head and saunters back inside.

"Can we go now?" Martin's voice brings me back to the car.

"Yeah, sure."

I start the engine, put the car in gear and start down the road past the club glaring at the front door. I watch through the rear-view window as the club disappears from my view.

CHAPTER 6

There are moments in life that define who we are and what we'll do. That night, in my car, sitting out in front of that club was a defining moment for me. Two months after that night with Martin, my sister's body turned up. She was barely recognizable. It was clear she was back on drugs and living a horrible existence the final few months of her life. The police classified it a suicide, but I knew better—it was a warning. To me. To Martin, and anyone else who thought they could take down Alistair and his brothers. I spent the next several years observing and learning everything there was to know about that club and the people who ran it.

Along the way I met many people involved in this life-style, the world of BDSM, but it never interested me. I became involved for very different reasons. Eventually, I found out the blond man that was having issues with Alistair that night was indeed a druggie. But, more importantly, he was also Landon's former roommate from college. There is more to that story, but Mr. Miller is a reserved man who keeps all his cards close to his chest, never revealing more than necessary. I knew something had happened to him that involved Alistair but had no details to go on. Whatever went on between the two, I knew it was much different from my story.

When Mr. Miller offered me a position at his club, I was tempted to turn him down. It was never my intention to work in these types of establishments for long, but there was something about Mr. Miller that was different than my other bosses. His intent never had anything to do with money and he is very big on safety in his place. He's not after the occasional abusive Dom. Mr. Miller is after so much more. So far, he's been reluctant to share his story with me and I respect his privacy. Don't get me wrong, I'm a little more than curious. At times over the years I've come close to asking, but his attitude about Alistair keeps me from bringing it up.

What I see in Mr. Miller is a man with the same agenda. A man ready to lie in wait until the time is right to strike. He is a patient man, far more patient than I. If I had my way, we would have struck long ago and probably botched any attempt to dismantle Alistair and his crew. Since joining forces with Mr. Miller, we have only gotten bigger and better. Then again, so has Alistair's business.

I believe one day soon everything I've been working towards will pay off. With Mr. Miller's help and resources, we'll both get what we have longed for. Until then, I will continue to work in the club, watching over the innocent people who don't know any better.

The lifestyle isn't for everyone. In fact, it's for a very distinct customer and owning this type of establishment comes with a lot of responsibilities.

Sliding the chair back from under the desk I stand and leave the monitors, heading over to my desk to get some work done. I left a pile of applications needing my attention from the previous day. It's uncharacteristic of me to leave work unfinished, but we had unforeseen circumstances in the club last night that delayed everything else. It's not often problems arise in the club, but occasionally, they do occur and are dealt with swiftly.

I once asked Mr. Miller why he sought me out, why he thought I would be a good match for his club. He replied, "It was your eyes. They held everything I needed to know."

I know exactly what he means because I felt the same way about him. For as cold as he can seem, his eyes hold a slight vulnerability, along with good old-fashioned revenge.

THE END

How far will you go to save a stranger?

With her marriage in shambles and life not turning out quite as she imagined, Alexandria turns to her best friend for help to snap her out of the slump that's been plaguing her. Instead she finds herself immersed in a world of danger, tangled in a web of deceit, and wrapped in the arms of an unattainable man. When an FBI investigation lands on her doorstep, she's dragged into a world of crime and punishment. With a club full of domineering men, she wonders who is trustworthy and who is capable of murder.

A shocking twist ending you won't believe...

The next book in the series: Control on Amazon

AUTHOR'S NOTE

When I thought about publishing my first novel, I asked myself several questions. *How could I do it? What is the best way to get my work into the world?* I admit, I tried to publish traditionally. Sending my query letters to about 15 Literary Agents. The results were not as depressing as I imagined them to be. When I researched how to query agents, the online writing community was of one mind... forget it. In fact, I was led to believe that winning the lottery would be easier than getting an agent and a published book. I received a few encouraging responses from the letters, but sadly no agent.

I sat on my book for the next four years as I entered college in the hopes of changing careers. My career choices before this time were not fulfilling and I wasn't living my dream. I raised my son and felt my life was becoming my own again. Actually, I thought, *'what do I have to lose,'* and it was that thought that allowed me to make the decision to leave everything behind and start a new life as a mature student. Best decision ever!

I entered a whole new world that taught me so much more than I could have hoped for and I took advantage of every opportunity available. College helped guide me to self-publishing. Once again, I was confronted with the question, *"what do I have to lose?"*

This book is written in the first person, is the story of a minor character from my novel and started out as a marketing ploy. I thought I was being smart writing a novella that would be an introduction to my true work. What a wonderful surprise this turned out to be. I had no idea when writing the novel this character would have such an intriguing story to tell. Don't get me wrong, I knew his character had a bigger role than what the novel portrayed. What I didn't know were the details of this character's life and the story he wanted to tell. Through writing this short tale I was able to see how important his character is to the plot in the novel and it was a lot more than I ever gave him credit for. And, that this marketing ploy—my brilliant idea—allowed me to understand my characters even better.

I am a big believer in timing—when the time is right, it will happen. Well, the time is right for Leroy to tell his story. I hope his journey is enough to inspire you to continue the expedition with me.

Renee

ABOUT THE AUTHOR

Constantly writing, R.M. Gauthier is always trying to produce new material. With two series under her belt and two more on the way, she will continue to work hard in order to bring her readers more of what they love. In the meantime, you can find all her works at the follow links:

Website
www.rmgauthier.com

Join R.M Gauthier's Newsletter a receive two free story!http://eepurl.com/dhB5xs

www.ingramcontent.com/pod-product-compliance
Lightning Source LLC
Chambersburg PA
CBHW070652130626
46555CB00006B/2844